For Elliot Jude Chaplin,
and for our beloved librarian
friends who share the love of
reading with all of us!
—A.S.C. and P.S.

I Can Read Book® is a trademark of HarperCollins Publishers.

ISBN 978-0-06-193507-7 (trade bdg.) — ISBN 978-0-06-193506-0 (pbk.)

13 14 15 16 17 SCP 10 9 8 7 6 5 4 3 2 1   ❖   First Edition

Biscuit Loves the Library

story by ALYSSA SATIN CAPUCILLI
pictures by PAT SCHORIES

HARPER
An Imprint of HarperCollinsPublishers

It's a very special day
at the library, Biscuit.
Woof, woof!

3

READ
TO A
PET DAY!

It's Read to a Pet Day!

I can read to you,

Biscuit.

Woof, woof!

Come along, Biscuit.

Let's find a book.

Woof, woof!

See, Biscuit?

There are books

about bunnies and bears.

Woof, woof!

And big dinosaurs, too!
Woof!

Funny puppy!

That's not a real bone!

Woof, woof!

Look, Biscuit.

There are more books

over here.

Woof, woof!

Biscuit! Where are you?

Woof!

You found the puppets,
Biscuit.

Woof, woof!
And you even found
stories we can listen to.
Woof!

Now, which book will it be?

Woof, woof!

Biscuit! Wait for me!

Woof!

Oh, Biscuit!

You found the librarian
and a book that's just right.
Woof, woof!

You found a cozy spot
filled with friends, too.

Everyone loves the library,
Biscuit.

Woof, woof!

Let's read!

Woof!